Corinne Davies

# Ralph is (*not*) a Superhero

Illustrated by

ALIS

_corinne_

**Corinne Davies** is both a playwright and writer
of children's poetry, who once met El on
a comedy course! She can also do the splits
and furthermore is both ginger and Welsh.

_el (or "L")_

**Eleanor Ashfield** is a freelance illustrator
and animator. She likes yoghurt (pronounced,
yugurt), frogs and spiders and rock'n'roll. Happily
umarried and living in Southernmost London.

_klara_

**Klara Smith** is a graphic designer and book artist
and does generally anything she can turn her
hand to. Keen on cats and boring films.

**Meet Ralph and listen to his story at: www. ralphisnotasuperhero.com**

# Chapters

# Chapter 1

## School and Dreams…and Stuff

Young Ralph was not that popular,
At school he had few friends.
He wasn't fast or good at sports,
But tried to make amends
By keeping out of people's way
And trying to be kind.
At break time he was always
Quite impossible to find.

He'd stay inside and read a book,
Or maybe practise chess.
For it might rain, or might be fine,
But Ralph could not care less.

He'd hide inside the library,
Until the bell would sound
As just outside the older boys
All threw themselves around.

At lunchtime he would sit alone,
And quickly scoff his food.
He'd smile at all the others,
As he hated being rude,
But kept his distance –
Burying his head inside a book.
The older boys would never
Give our Ralph a second look.

Ralph's sister found him bothersome
And terribly un-cool.
She tried to just ignore him
If their paths should cross at school.

10

'So where's your swotty brother?'
All the older girls would ask.
She tried, in vain, to get poor Ralph
To always wear a mask!

But then one night Ralph had a dream, that turned his world around.

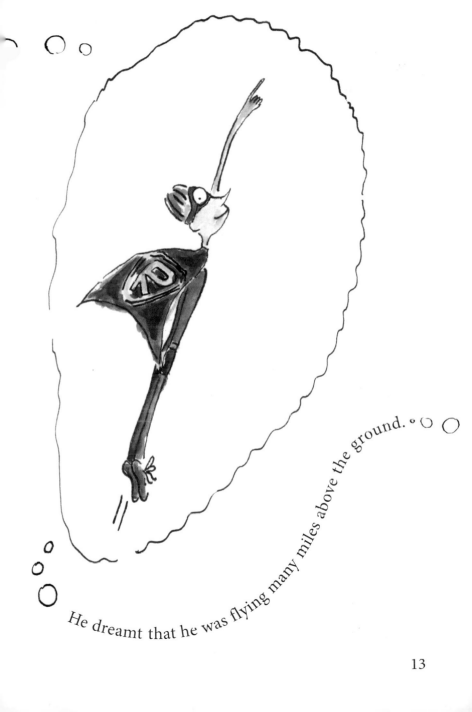

He dreamt that he was flying many miles above the ground.

He fought with baddies, rescued pets,

Was brave and super strong...

And woke up in a sweat and questioned if his dream was wrong.

"Last night I dreamt I was a superhero!"
Ralph declared,
(Arriving down for breakfast,
as his older sister glared.)

'So what's your uniform like Ralph
– in red, or maybe blue?'

"Don't laugh at me!"
Said Ralph
"Or else I'll use
My powers on YOU!"

Ralph's sister walked out laughing
And his mother shook her head.

'Your special powers are only real
When you're asleep in bed.'

"But mum, I flew and walked
Through walls and I was pretty cool!"

'That's great,' replied Ralph's mum,
'But now it's time to go to school!'

'Now class, you all must listen for tomorrow there will be,
A poetry competition, and I need your help, you see.
Together we must choose the person
Whom we all think best,

To represent our class and
To annihilate the rest!'

"I'll volunteer to read!" said Ralph,
The class all turned, surprised.
'You hate to read.' 'But you're too quiet and useless Ralph!'
they cried.

"I know that I can do this, miss,
If you give me the chance!"

And Ralph arose,
Adopting his new superhero stance.

# Chapter 2

## Don't Look Up!

H is mottled knees were knocking,
And his lips had turned bright blue.
Ralph stood upon the platform,
And surveyed the faces who…
Were staring back –
Amazed that Ralph would ever face them all.
Five hundred faces packed into
The large assembly hall.

"I AM a superhero!"
Whispered Ralph,
with startled eyes.
"And with my super powers
I know that I can win this prize!"

He gazed ahead, and briefly
Was transfixed by his reflection,
As all his classmates glared
Towards their teacher's strange selection.

But then a heavy
thundering noise
Was heard above Ralph's head.
(As Ralph was on his final
verse, he shouted it instead.)

'Look out!' screamed poor Ralph's teacher,
As the noise became a roar.
Then suddenly the ceiling came down crashing to the floor!

The Head cried out 'Where's Ralph?'
as he picked plaster from his stubble.
'He's here!' replied one teacher.
'In that Ralph-shaped pile of rubble.

He's dead, he has to be –
those ceiling tiles must weigh a tonne.
It's tragic that poor Ralph was killed
before his verse was done!'

'Quick, someone call an ambulance
…his parents…and the nurse!
Explain that Ralph was sadly crushed
mid-way through final verse.

I guess by now he's realised
he's got no super powers.
But still, he died so bravely
– oh, and get his mum some flowers!'

With that, a distant mumbling
 Came from the rubble stack.
  A hand emerged, and then
   A foot came poking through the back.

Then finally
 Ralph's head was seen,
 Intact, but slightly dusty.
'He IS a superhero…but his powers are clearly rusty!'

"I'm not a superhero...

        I'm just Ralph...now can't you see!
I'm lucky, that was all,

        that nothing heavy fell on me.
I thought that I had special powers...

        but clearly was mistaken,
It's just because I ducked in time,

        that's all that saved my bacon!"

'Perhaps he wasn't lying,'
Ralph's mum whispered in the car.
'Well not about the flying,
As he's not done that so far...
But no one could survive
That type of thing and feel no pain.'
'I know!' replied his dad,
As he reversed into their lane.

'But he's no superhero – he's too young –
And goes to school.
I'm sure that superheroes
Rarely do that as a rule.
Besides, our Ralph wears glasses,
And he cannot fly or see,
With that super x-ray vision –
He's short-sighted, just like me!'


'But superheroes come in many forms,
                              like in the books
They usually disguise themselves
                    with common, normal looks,
Just like our Ralph!
                    Perhaps he has a special flying cape
On underneath his uniform
                    …and fixed with special tape.'

# Chapter 3

## Cat's Overhead!

The next day, back at school,
Our Ralph enjoyed a sudden fame.
'That's superhero Ralph!' they cried,
'It's really such a shame,
That we ever thought to doubt him,
For there's nothing he can't do.
I bet he walks through walls –
Or disappears in front of you!'

Though Ralph still questioned
Whether all his super powers were real.
Despite the ceiling incident,
He knew he didn't feel
Like he thought a superhero should –
So confident and bold.
But usually they're not called Ralph,
Or only eight years old!

And little things kept happening,
Which seemed a little strange.
He'd kick a ball, or throw a stick, beyond his usual range.

And all around were witnesses,
To note Ralph's transformation.
(He even answered questions on his local radio station!)

But three days later, walking home from school,
To Ralph's surprise,
He found a small girl blubbering
With red and swollen eyes.

At first he thought he'd walk on by,
Not offering his assistance,
As some folk that he'd tried to help
Had met him with resistance.

"What's wrong?" said Ralph.

The little girl just stood there, so upset.

'Some boys have thrown my cat into that tree
just for a bet!'

"I'll call the fire brigade," Ralph said.

"And see what they can do."

'They're stuck in traffic', said the girl,
'So now it's up to YOU!'

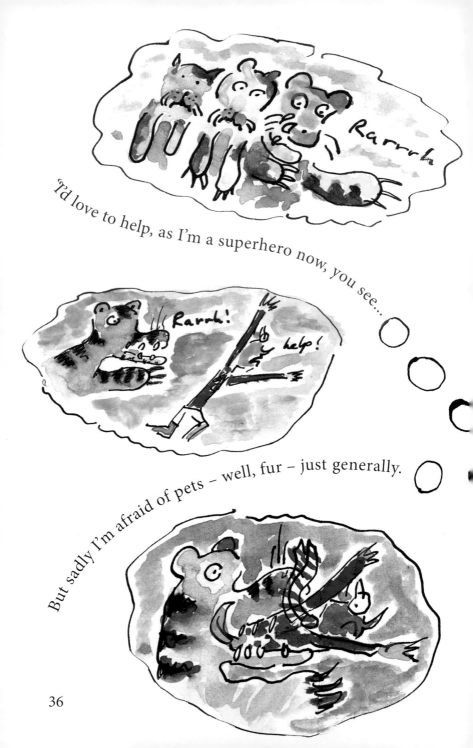

'I'd love to help, as I'm a superhero now, you see...

But sadly I'm afraid of pets – well, fur – just generally.

36

I haven't tried to fly yet – oh, plus I'm afraid of heights,
All ever since the football team
        Once tied me to their kites!"

'But you're a superhero – you're the only one to help!'
As suddenly her cat gave out an awful, high-pitched yelp!
"I really think I should explain: there's limits to my powers!"
'You'll have to climb!' the girl replied.
'They won't be here for hours!'

So Ralph whipped off his blazer,
And began to climb the tree.
The leaves and swaying branches
Made it hard for him to see.
'The breeze is getting stronger!'
cried the little girl in awe...
Then suddenly Ralph's glasses
Landed shattered on the floor.

But then a sudden gust of wind
Caught Ralph quite unaware.
The cat climbed upwards to Ralph's head
And nestled in his hair.
"It's just too strong...I can't hold on!"
– Was poor Ralph's final plea.
As finally the two were blown
Directly off the tree!

'I say him FLY!…I saw him FLY!'
The girl cried in delight.
'I've not seen someone FLY before!
– I'll never sleep tonight!

And now my cat is famous too!'
– The people gathered round.
While Ralph checked all his arms
and legs had also reached the ground.

"I'm not convinced I really FLEW!"
Ralph said to one reporter.
'HE DID!' the girl's dad stated,
As he posed beside his daughter.

"It might have been that I was BLOWN…
I'm sorry but it's true.
Without an action replay, I can't really say I FLEW!"

'This boy is just so modest!'
all the local papers said.
Poor Ralph just mulled it over
as he lay awake in bed.

The next day, back at school,
He wished he'd never had that dream…
As heading straight towards him came
The *dreaded* football team!

# Chapter 4

The *Dreaded* Football Team…and Ivy

'So you're a superhero, Ralph?'
The Captain mocked aloud.
'Well we've a space upon the team –
I know that you'll be proud,
To play this afternoon in this:
Our last match of the season.
For if you play we cannot lose...
And that's our basic reason!'

"I'd love to play – I really would!"
Said Ralph, now feeling dizzy.
"It really would be great fun...but I'm sadly rather busy."

'Too busy for the football team?'

    The Captain scoffed and jeered.

        One hour later,

            Ralph was on the pitch,

                Just as he feared.

            'Now get stuck in!'

         The Captain yelled,

      'Your strip's still gleaming white!'

"I know!" said Ralph,

"But I don't need to have a bath tonight!"

'Look out!' cried one spectator,

As poor Ralph began to fall...

He didn't see it coming, till his head bounced off the ball!

'It's superhero Ralph!' –
The team began to scream his name,
As the final whistle sounded, thereby finishing the game.
'It's true! He scored the winning goal!'
The boys cried out in awe.
Then screamed and
Jumped on top of
Him and threw
Him to the
Floor.


"Don't
Kill me!"
Shouted Ralph.
"Besides…I just don't
Have the time. I've got to
Go to chess club now, and they'll
Report your crime!" 'Ralph…no one
Wants to kill you! You're a hero, don't you see?'
"That's great – but could you tell these boys –
They're really squashing me!"

'You'll have to join our team now, Ralph.'
The Captain gave the sign.
And Ralph was hoisted in the air,
Above the half way line.

"It's weird this superhero thing"
Ralph told his mum at tea.
"They all forget that I'm still Ralph –
I'm normal – I'm just ME!"

The next weekend, Ralph ventured out
To buy himself a treat.
He didn't think he'd need his powers
Just walking down the street.

But noticed one old lady –
As her shopping bags had burst.
So being Ralph he thought he'd better help
    her with them first.

'Ahh – you're that superhero – yes I saw you in the papers.
I read about your exploits and your people-saving capers.

It's great that in this day and age,

There's people like yourself

To care for us old ladies –

      not just leave us on the shelf!'

"Perhaps," said Ralph "I'll visit you,
…I could come after school –
Except on Thursday evenings,
When I've chess club as a rule!"

'I'd really love it if you would!'
The lady took his arm,
'Being round a superhero
I just feel so very calm!'

And true to word –
Ralph visited old Ivy every week.
He'd stay for tea and biscuits,
Whilst for hours and hours they'd speak…

Of school…and books…and other things,
Both new and often dated.
Whilst Ralph explained he found
His new-found status overrated.

"It's like I'm some celebrity or something!"
Ralph explained.
"It's really quite a pressure
And I'm feeling slightly drained!"
'It must be, you poor darling!' stated Ivy, offering cake.
"I know that someday soon," Ralph said

        "I'll make some big mistake!"

# Chapter 5

## The Rude Man

One afternoon Ralph realised
The time had surely come,
To count up all his coppers
And to bank their princely sum.

He placed them in a big glass jar
Then headed down the road.
And waited by the crossing
With his shiny, heavy load.

With that a car came screeching past,
Then jammed its breaks on tight.
Ralph watched the driver closely
As he started to alight.

He grabbed a briefcase quickly,
As he flung his door out wide.
But walking past Ralph noticed
That he'd left his keys inside.

"Your keys!" Ralph shouted to the man

Who'd reached the big bank doors.

"You left them in your car,

So I'm assuming

These are

Yours

!"


'I

Left

Them there

Deliberately you fool!'

The man replied. Then rudely

Grabbed them from Ralph's hand,

and quickly fled inside

.

"How odd!" Ralph muttered quietly,
As he joined the shortest bank queue.
You really would have thought he could
At least have said 'GOSH, THANK YOU' "

'Some people are so rude!'
Agreed the lady to his right.
'And parking in a 'NO PARK ZONE'
Is really not polite!'

A passing clerk surveyed young Ralph,
Approaching with a smile,
'That jar must be quite heavy –
You'll be queuing for a while.'

"I saved these up for charity,"
Ralph told the clerk with pride.
'Then bring them over here to me!'
The kindly clerk replied.

But as Ralph's jar was just so large,
His view was pretty poor…
And he didn't see the handbag
Someone left upon the floor.

Before he knew it Ralph had tripped, his jar flew through the air...

Then smashed upon the floor – its contents flying everywhere!

Oi, You!…Where are the toilets?'
Said the rude man from outside.

'We don't have any here,
Now PLEASE WATCH OUT!'
The clerk replied.

'No toilets here!' the rude man boomed,
'That's no use, is it sonny?'

– But he'd ignored the man's advice
And skidded on the money.

The briefcase did three somersaults...

Then burst on crashing down.

A silence then descended,

With the clerk the first to frown.

'SECURITY!' the clerk yelled out
'THIS MAN MUST BE RESTRAINED!'
And glanced, once more – still open-mouthed
At what the case contained...

One black eye-mask,
One stripy top,
Some gloves
And
One toy gun,
    One toothbrush,
        Bag
            And passport,
For his new life on the run!

But if that wasn't bad enough,
        Ralph pointed at the bag!
As on it, in bold lettering,
    Four letters spelled out 'SWAG'.

"He must have planned to change here in the toilets!"
Ralph declared.
'It's all YOUR fault I failed!'
The rude man yelled, with nostrils flared.

"That's why his keys were in the car!
So he could leave at speed."
'It all makes sense!' the clerk replied,
(Still following Ralph's lead.)

Security had called, so the police were on their way.
A crowd had gathered round poor Ralph,
Who felt obliged to say…

"… I dropped those coins by accident!"
'No, Ralph!' the clerk began,
'You used your SUPER powers
To foil that rude man's evil plan!'

"No really," Ralph replied
"You see – I'm clumsy – nothing more!
And that's the only reason
All my coins were on the floor."

'You saw the FUTURE,' said the clerk
'And knew what you must do!'
'IT'S HIM AGAIN!!'
– Ralph turned to greet his local TV crew.

# Chapter 6

## One too many Brussels!

So poor Ralph had to just accept,
It wasn't safe to go:
To school, the bank, or football games,
Where everyone would know...
About his so-called 'super powers'
– Instead our Ralph decided,
To nip down to the library,
Where his favourite books resided.

He headed to his favourite aisle,
With books on playing chess.
But on arrival noticed
All the books were in a mess.
Ralph thought this most unusual,
And hurried off at pace,
To find the man responsible
– His old friend, Mr. Grace.

"Where's Mr. Grace today?"
Ralph asked a lady passing by.
"This section's in an awful mess...
I'm forced to question why?

His shelves are always spotless,

So imagine my surprise…

On finding three books

Wrongly filed,

One sock…

And two

Mince

Pies

!"

'I must apologise, Ralph,
But the truth is somewhat weird:
Our lifelong friend and colleague,
Mr. Grace, has disappeared!

He left this list three weeks ago,
Of chess books you should borrow
– They're putting an appeal out
On the local news tomorrow.'


Ralph took his books and headed off,
Debating any reason,
His friend might take an unexpected
Holiday off-season.

Perhaps a relative was ill?…perhaps he'd won the lotto?
For 'Go to work, and then play chess!'
                    Was Mr. Grace's motto.

Distracted by his thoughts,
Ralph took a wrong turn walking home,
And found some old allotments
(Where he wouldn't normally roam!)

The sheds looked old and musty
And the soil was full of weeds.
(Except for one allotment,
Sporting newly planted seeds.)

Ralph turned to leave,
But heard a noise and quickly spun around.
"Who's there?" he shouted out,
Then heard a second banging sound.

Ralph glanced towards the tidy shed,
Then edged a little nearer.
And thought the faint 'Help!'
That he'd heard was slowly
Getting clearer...

'Ralph!' the faint voice shouted out
  'You found me here, at last!
  You'll have to get the fire brigade
– They've got to get here fast.
A tree has blocked the door way,
I've been stuck here for three weeks...
Surviving on a diet of cabbage, carrots, sprouts and leeks!'

"Mr. Grace!" Ralph started
"Are you hurt, are you in pain?"
'Just bloated, Ralph…' the voice replied
'…And trying to stay sane!

The first week wasn't bad,
But things have gone down-hill from there.
With all the sprouts I've eaten,
There's a shortage of clean air!'


"Wait!" Ralph shouted out
"I'll bring some help to move this tree!"
'Please call an ambulance as well,
As Ralph you're soon to see…

A diet of just vegetables
Means now I'm somewhat rounded.
With all this gas inside me,
It's quite hard just staying grounded!'

The fire brigade had moved the tree,
But then were forced instead,
To sadly lift the roof
From poor old
Mr. Grace's
Shed.

The
Smell was
Rather pungent,
So their masks had been
Applied, because of all the built up
Gas the shed contained
Inside.

And Mr. Grace came floating out,
Just like a giant balloon.
With swollen arms and legs
– His face a round and bloated moon.

The ambulance men tried in vain
To get him through their doors.
But had to leave them open
And give up on this lost cause!

'I'll be fine soon, don't worry!'
Mr. Grace began to say,
'This boy is such a HERO!'
– Then they slowly drove away.

'He used his x-ray hearing
And he heard my frightened plea!'
"Oh not again!…" poor Ralph replied
"…I'm normal, I'm just ME!"

# Chapter 7

## Ralph Gets the Girl
## (and more from Ivy)

N ow Ralph was not allowed to walk
His sister home from school.
(She made him walk quite far behind,
And never bent this rule!)

This day she walked with Amy,
On whom Ralph had quite a crush.
Whenever Amy passed him,
Poor old Ralph would always blush.

He tried to catch them up,
So he could listen to them talking.
He wished he really *could* fly,
As he couldn't reach them walking!

But he could overhear just parts of what his sister said,
Above the traffic noises that were
Buzzing round his head.

'He's not a superhero – he's embarrassing – that's all!
This all began that day inside our school assembly hall.
Now everybody thinks he's great – a hero!
– What a laugh!
It's not just all the children,
But now all the teaching
Staff!'

'You must admit' said Amy,
  'He's performed amazing feats!
    I never noticed him before,
      Now everyone he meets
        Has heard of him…you should be proud
          Of all these debts he's owed!'
            But listening to her friend,
              Ralph's sister stepped into the road!

"LOOK OUT!"
  Ralph threw his sister
    From the pathway of the car.
      The impact tossed him in the air
        And threw him pretty far…
          From where his sister landed,
            Just surveying what occurred.
              The ambulance's siren
                Was the last thing poor Ralph heard!

He soon awoke in hospital, with Ivy at his side.
His sister had to leave,
Each time she looked at him, she cried!

He'd broken arms and legs –
And what was left was cut and bruised!
(At least they'd left a TV set to keep poor Ralph amused.)

Ralph turned to Ivy
(Plaster-casts prevented moving much!)
But tried to reach her fingers, with a friendly little touch.

"I'll tell you this in person, as I didn't want to call,
But it turns out that I'm NOT a superhero after all!"

'I know, dear!' stated Ivy,
 As she eyed his sweets with glee.
'But still you're such a SPECIAL boy –
You've been so kind to me.

You're not of superhero stock,
But when you thought you were…
Then you were bold and brave and strong
– And less afraid of fur!'

"What use am I to anyone
Without my super powers?"
'You never had those Ralph, my dear!'
She said, arranging flowers.

'Yet when you thought you MIGHT have had,
Remember how that felt?
It made you strong and fearless,
Having that under your belt!'

A few weeks later, Ralph was told to go back home to rest.

(The nurses were not fond of chess,

so they all thought it best.)

He stood, in shock, outside his house

On slightly swollen feet.

As banners and balloons were littered

All around the street...

WELCOME RALPH OUR HERO!

Said the banner near his head,

WE DON'T NEED SUPERHEROES HERE

WE'VE GOT YOU INSTEAD!

Then Amy wandered over and
Kissed Ralph upon the cheek.
When she asked to be his girlfriend –
Well, poor Ralph could hardly speak!


Eventually the crowds had left
And Ralph collapsed at last.
His sister even wrote a note upon his plaster cast.
　　　　　　　　　　　　And Ivy sat down,
　　　　　　　Next to Ralph, and gave a secret wink.
　　　　　　　　'You see they like you anyway…
　　　　　　　　　　No matter what you think!'


"…I think I really knew my powers
Were only in my mind!"
'Oh no, dear…all your powers are REAL,
Just…of a different kind!
　　　　　For everyone's a superhero – in their special way
　　　　　　　　It's how we choose to USE our powers,
　　　　　　　　　　That guides us on our way!'

# The End